A Story for Isabel

Wewer Keohane

A STORY FOR ISABEL

 Oneirica is a Registered Trademark

https://www.createspace.com/3408181

Cover Art: "Isabel's Pillow #3" by Wewer Keohane
Library of Congress Cataloging-in-publication data has been applied for. ISBN 1449580319

EAN-13 9781449580315

Inside photo by Steve Keohane

Created in the United States of America

10 9 8 7 6 5 4 3 2 1

A Story for Isabel

Wewer Keohane

This book is dedicated to my

grandaughters:

Indigo & Raven.

And, of course, to Isabel.

A Story for Isabella by Wewer Keohane

Dogs offer the precious opportunity, even
to people who are trapped in their egos, of
loving and being loved unconditionally.

Eckhart Tolle

A Story for Isabel

By Wewer Keohane

Jesse looked out the living room window at the lightly falling snow. She and Isabel had just come in from a wet walk and Jesse was ready for a good read. As she opened her book, Isabel came up beside her and nuzzled her arm. Jesse mindlessly petted Isabel's head. It wasn't enough for Isabel. She scratched the side of the sofa, a strong clue that she wanted something from Jesse.

"We just went for a walk girl. What do you want now?"

"Woof, rrrrrr," said Isabel.

"Are you hungry?" Jesse asked. But Isabel just stared at her.

"Tell me with one of your pillows, girl."

A Story for Isabella by Wewer Keohane

Isabel trotted over to her living room bed and picked out her bone pillow with the giraffe hide pattern.

"Ah," said Jesse. "You don't want me to read, do you? You want me to tell you your favorite story."

"Woof!"

"Okay, you spoiled rotten, beautiful creature, you. Get up here with me and I will tell you the story of Bear and Isabella." Isabel pulled herself onto the sofa and cuddled next to Jesse, putting her nose just barely on Jesse's thigh and sighed. And Jesse began to tell her their favorite story.

Once upon a time there was a dog named Bear. He was called Bear because he looked like one. His ears were too small for his big head, his toenails were overgrown and he smelled quite musty. And he was found in bear country.

When Jesse and Max saw him lying in the driveway, they couldn't imagine where he'd come from. They hadn't seen him before and they didn't see anyone around. As Jesse approached him she noticed blood on his front paws. He was gentle and trusting as she looked at his back paws, also bloody.

Jesse and Max's driveway is about a quarter mile long, jutting off a country road that's paved and all Jesse and Max could conclude was Bear had run on that hot paved road – it was the fourth of July – until he'd burned the skin off his paws. Bear must have instinctually headed down their road toward the creek and soft grasses.

Jesse called the local radio stations and newspapers and took Bear to Dr. Ben, the vet who tended to their four cats. Dr. Ben bandaged Bear's feet after hydrating him. He didn't recognize Bear so Max took some photos to post at other veterinarian offices and the rescue centers.

Dr. Ben put enough padding in Bear's bandages so that Bear could walk slowly. He told Jesse to give Bear a couple days of rest before she began walking him again.

A Story for Isabella by Wewer Keohane

Living in the country, Jesse and Max had no need to hit pavement to hike. Soft ground led to their pond and beyond into the woods. Bear and Jesse started out slowly to see how he faired. Their daily walks seemed to cheer him up. He was well behaved and affectionate and didn't bark, nor did he seem nervous. He was a sweet and calm presence.

Jesse and Max had planned a trip down the Grand Canyon over July fourth, but for some reason Jesse could only describe as intuition, they just hadn't wanted to go when the time came. Jesse realized now that had they gone, they would have missed the opportunity to nurture Bear, who quickly became dear to their hearts.

Jesse bought Bear a fake bear rug to sleep on, a red collar and leash set with little bears embroidered in black, good food and some toys. Days went by with no word from anyone or news from the media.

Then a call came. A family who lived a few miles away had been on vacation, leaving their dog with a neighbor. The neighbor had taken the dog for a ride in the back of his truck and when he got to his destination he was dogless! Bear's owners missed him. His name was Roger. They wanted him back. Could they come over and pick him up? Jesse wondered if Roger preferred being called Bear.

Many thoughts came to Max and Jesse: Were RogerBear's owners irresponsible for leaving Bear with the neighbors....did they love Bear like Max and Jesse did?

When RogerBear heard his original family's truck coming down the drive, his ears perked. When he saw the kids, he began trotting toward them. Max and Jesse, as much as they wanted to, could not keep Bear from this lovely family who he'd grown up with and who missed him. His name wasn't Bear and he did not belong to Max and Jesse.

The house felt empty. Why had we gone without a dog for so long, Jesse wondered. The pain of losing their dogs so many years ago was no longer a good enough reason to go without one now. Max agreed.

Jesse closed her eyes and saw a white female dog with perky ears and a beautiful face filled with huge brown-gold eyes. That's the dog I will look for, she thought.

At this point in the story Jesse looked down at Isabel, still resting her chin on Jesse's lap. Her heart opened every time she came to this part of the story. Isabel looked up at her and squeezed her eyebrows together, wondering why Jesse had stopped the story.

"Okay, girl," Jesse said. "I'll continue."

The next day as Jesse thumbed through the newspapers, there she was. In the Animal Rescue ads there was a picture of the beautiful white dog she had imagined. She was looking straight at Jesse saying "please". By noon Jesse was meeting her at the parking lot next to the mini mart. By 12:15p.m. Jesse had written a donation check for $75 and gotten very defined instructions and history from a woman who was clearly concerned about the dog's future.

A Story for Isabella by Wewer Keohane

Coyote had been adopted and returned to the center many times because no one felt they could train her. She was scared to death of people. She'd run away if not leashed. Jesse let all the information wash over her. She knew this was "her" dog. She felt it. She took Coyote to the car and let her sit in the front seat with her. Jesse reached over and held Coyote's beautiful little white face in her hands. Coyote's big brown eyes stared right into Jesse's green ones.

"You're too beautiful to be called Coyote," Jesse said. Your name is going to be Isabella and I am going to dedicate myself to helping you feel loved and to be free. Will you cooperate with me?"

Isabella was still looking Jesse in the eye. Jesse moved her hands to Isabella's ears and rubbed inside them and scratched the back of them. She slipped Isabella a little treat – sliced roast beef. Isabella was remarkably gentle taking the meat from Jesse. Jesse scratched Isabella's forehead as Isabella curled up on the seat and sighed.

A Story for Isabella by Wewer Keohane

Isabella weighed in at 40 pounds. Dr. Ben had no idea what breed she was. "Maybe a little Husky in her," he said. She needed to gain some weight. He thought she would be less shy after time with Jesse.

As soon as Jesse showed Isabella where her food and water was and took off her leash, Isabella found her way into the bedroom at the back of the house and slipped into the closet under Max's shirts. Max nor Jesse could get her to come out without leashing her and pulling her.

She pulled on the leash when Jesse walked her. When outside on a staked lead, Isabella would hide in the lilac bushes, getting tangled. It broke Jesse's heart that Isabella wasn't warming up to her as she had hoped. She was eating and would even jump up on Max and Jesse's bed to be with them, but she would stay at their feet. She only liked being touched when she was in the car with Jesse. Isabella, although over a year old, had never been house broken so Jesse took her everywhere with her in the car, which Isabella seemed to like. She didn't mind waiting for Max and Jesse in the car whereas she would pace and pant if Jesse left her at home even if Max was there. She slowly became attached to Jesse but she wouldn't let Max near her, even barking at him if he was carrying something, and she shied away from other people.

When Max drove, Isabella would sit on the floor in front of Jesse and put her head on Jesse's knee. She started following Jesse wherever she went and responded to the words "walk" and "ride". Jesse taught Isabella to stop as soon as she heard a car on the road when they were walking, but Jesse couldn't trust her off leash. Isabella would run right back home and hide in the lilac bushes once again.

Jesse was saddened by what seemed to be Isabella's lack of trust toward her. She felt Isabella was still afraid Max and Jesse were going to return her to her cage at the rescue center.

About a month after having Isabella and doing little but caring for her, Max and Jesse decided to go to a lecture in the town about thirty miles east of them. "Isabel-la, Isabel-la, she's the best , most beautiful,

A Story for Isabella by Wewer Keohane

wonderful girl in the world." Jesse and Max sang chorus after chorus of their love song to Isabella on the drive in, hoping it would relax her and make her feel loved.

When they arrived at the lecture, they were surprised that valet service was required and they told the valet they had to park the car themselves as Isabella would be too scared if someone else got in the car with her. The valet let them park and told them to leave the keys in the car.

Jesse had an odd feeling in her gut and found it hard to focus during the lecture. She wished they had not followed the valet's instructions and had locked the car. As the lecture ended, a valet approached Max, asking if he was the owner of the silver SUV. Jesse jumped out of her seat. "What, what's happened to my girl?"

"We're sorry, ma'am, but one of our valets went to put literature in your car and your dog jumped out. We chased him and chased him but he kept running."

"She. Isabella's a she! Show me where! Why didn't you come and get us immediately?" Jesse was infuriated, grief stricken . Panic rose up her body. She was afraid she had lost Isabella forever and worried that her shyness would prevent anyone from catching her. Max and Jesse roamed the fields near the site of the lecture for hours, calling Isabella, weeping, holding each other.

Fortunately, Max and Jesse had taken some great pictures of their beautiful girl and they spent days posting photos and posters, running ads on the radio and in newspapers. Only two calls of sightings came in and they had no luck following them up. They spent a night near one of the locations and thought they saw Isabella but if it was her, she wouldn't come to them. This created even more anguish.

Everyone who'd met Isabella wanted to win her over. Many people thought her shyness was because she must be a wolf. She did look like one. Maybe that's why her original name was Coyote. Jesse and Max's friends, after a week of witnessing their searching and grieving, began to tell them:"She's a wild animal, she doesn't want to be domesticated. Let her go. Maybe she's found her pack."

On the eighth night of Isabella being gone, Jesse prayed that she could let go and that Isabella would be happy and safe without her. She could not remember having ever grieved so much. She was exhausted with worry. Her grief was so deep; as deep as when she'd lost a loved one to death. The sleep she got was from sheer exhaustion. "I feel so scared for her," she told Max.

About 9 a.m. the next morning, a Friday, the phone rang. "If I hadn't read the paper this morning and seen that picture of that dog, I would have shot her," the gruff voice said. "I thought she was a wolf or a coyote. (He pronounced it ky-ōt.) She's still hanging around my hay bales. Won't come near me. That red collar made me look twice." Thank God she had on her collar, Jesse thought.

The rancher gave Jesse directions. She called Max, who was out on a job, and an animal control officer she had previously asked for help. She had never driven so far so fast or in such little time. The three of them rendezvoused near the hay bales. The river was just below them and the officer went down to look around. Max and Jesse called and called, "Isabella, Isabella."

They had no luck. Eventually, Max had to go back to work and the officer moved on. Jesse was staying put. Overnight if necessary, she told Max. She opened the car doors in case Isabella came to the car while she was searching. She took the roast beef she had remembered to bring with her.

Jesse began walking the perimeter of the bales calling "Isabella, Isabella, I love you girl. Please come. Come to your Mama." She went back to the car. No luck. She walked toward the bales to begin walking in between them again, calling.

Then, through two huge round bales, there she came, skinny, with her head down low, just slinking toward Jesse. Jesse squatted to be on Isabella's level and as Isabella approached she put her head between Jesse's knees and nuzzled her. She looked up and Jesse got her very first

A Story for Isabella by Wewer Keohane

Isabella lick. Right on the mouth. Heaven. Jesse gave her some roast beef and Isabella gulped it and licked Jesse's hands. Isabella hopped in the car without a leash. As Jesse got into the driver's seat Isabella scrunched over and put her head in Jesse's lap and kept it there while Jesse gave her the rest of the roast beef. She stayed on Jesse's lap all the way home.

Isabella has never again hidden in the closet or under the lilac bushes, nor needed a leash or a stake with a lead. She never goes across Jesse and Max's land boundaries without them. She is with Jesse always now, the most loyal and loving and well behaved animal Jesse ever hoped to befriend. Isabella has gained 30 pounds, and even licks the hands of friends. She has many buddies at the dog park and up the road. Jesse knows that Isabella appreciates Jesse for not giving up on her and Jesse's heart warms when she sees how Isabella is now able to give and receive love. The End

Isabel's head was still resting on Jesse's thigh and her breath was steady. Her eyes were closed and she had a puffy little smile that Jesse and Max always chuckled over. It was a smile of contentment, with her upper lip puffy, as if it were stuffed with cotton, hung over her lower lip and the dark black line turned upward.

A Story for Isabella by Wewer Keohane

Proof

Made in the USA